This Little Tiger book belongs to:

....

....

....

Stella J Jones

Judi Abbot

GLITTER

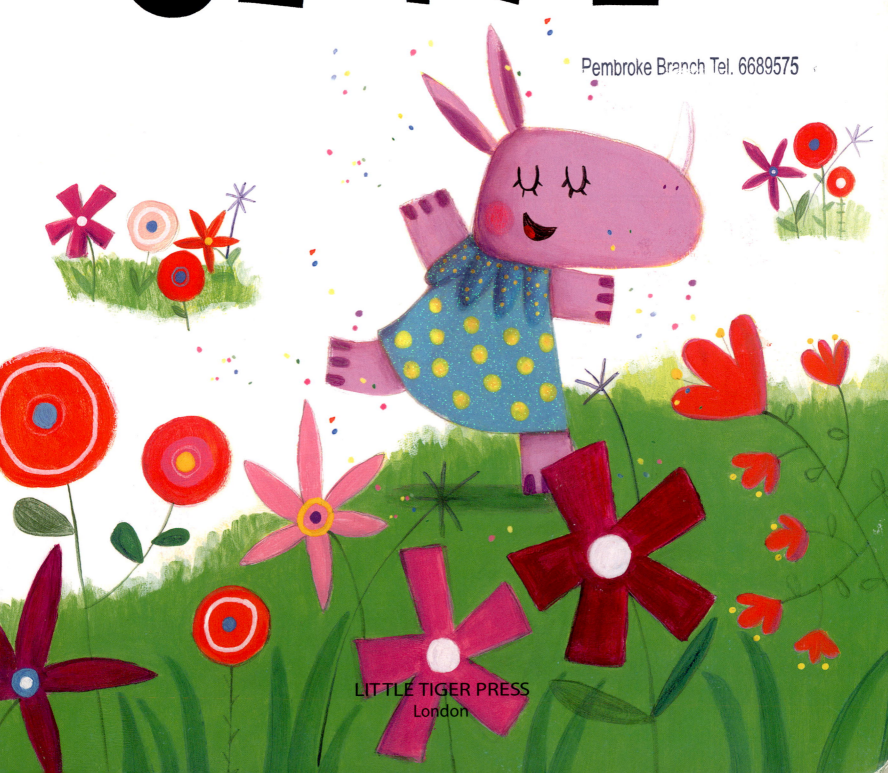

LITTLE TIGER PRESS
London

There was once a little rhino called Gloria.
And Gloria's favourite colour was

glitter!

Which is **bonkers** because everyone
knows glitter isn't a real colour.
But did Gloria care? Not on your nelly!

Everything in her life
had a little bit of
razzle-dazzle.

She had spangle pants,
glitter slippers,

and a
glitzerama-
razzamatazz
scooter!

And everywhere Gloria went she left a little bit of glittery happiness behind her.

Just

like

this.

She **glittered** the banker,

the barber, the baker.

She **dazzled** the chef

and the furniture-maker!

She **glitzed** up the plumbers,

she **spangled** the drummers,

she **spritzed** up the teachers and the long-distance runners.

Don't they look **glorious**?!

Don't they look **happy**?!

Actually, they don't look
very happy, do they?

This is awkward.

"No more glitter, Gloria!"
they all called after the little rhino.
But did Gloria hear them? No she did not!

There was only one thing to do –
scrub that glitter off!

But (as everyone knows) once glorious glitter
gets out of the pot

it goes everywhere!

uh-oh.

SPOILER ALERT

It's about to get **messy!**

Barney the architect **bumped** into Fred,

who **ran** into Holly and Molly – **how jolly!**

Harry **hugged** Larry,

who **shook paws** with Gary,

who **high-fived** and **fist-bumped** both Sally and Barry!

Soon Gloria's glitter had covered
the **whole town!**

There was some on the **tower**
and **lots** on the **steeple,**
as well as the **market**
and all of the **people.**

Even Pa Elephant
looked rather
glum . . .

... because he'd got **glitter** all over **his bum!**

Cripes. If they were grumpy before they're going to be **really angry** now!

Close your ears, this is about **to get shouty!**

Ooh, cheeky!

But instead of all **Shouting** and **Stomping** and **Snorting**, there was **tittering**, **giggling**, **chuckling** and **chortling!**

Just like the glitter that spread up and down,
The **happiness** travelled right through the town!

Phew! Everyone loves a happy ending!

Hooray for Gloria!

She made a whole town smile with her
razzle-dazzle!

And even though it's clear to see that glitter STILL
isn't a real colour, did Gloria care?

Not on your nelly!

For Meliha, whose favourite colour is glitter ~ S J

For Virginia, who is always glittery ~ J A

LITTLE TIGER PRESS

1 The Coda Centre, 189 Munster Road, London SW6 6AW

www.littletiger.co.uk

First published in Great Britain 2017
This edition published 2017

Text by Stella J Jones
Text copyright © Little Tiger Press 2017
Illustrations copyright © Judi Abbot 2017
Judi Abbot has asserted her right to be identified as the author and illustrator of
this work under the Copyright, Designs and Patents Act, 1988

A CIP catalogue record for this book is available from the British Library

All rights reserved • 978-1-84869-432-3

Printed in China • LTP/1800/1654/0816

2 4 6 8 10 9 7 5 3 1

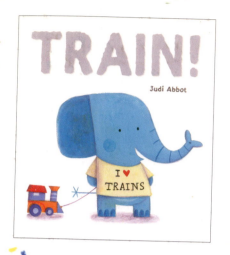

TRAIN!
Judi Abbot

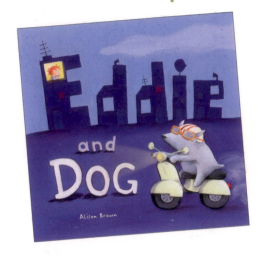

Eddie and DOG
Alison Brown

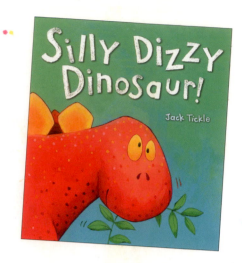

Silly Dizzy Dinosaur!
Jack Tickle

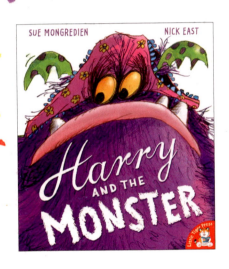

SUE MONGREDIEN NICK EAST
Harry AND THE MONSTER

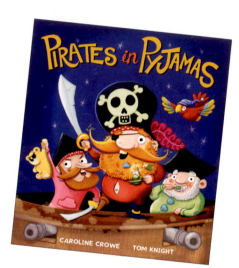

PiRATES in PyJAMAS
CAROLINE CROWE TOM KNIGHT

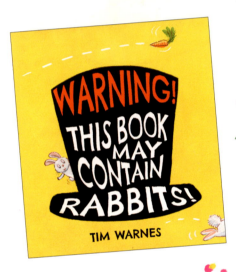

WARNING! THIS BOOK MAY CONTAIN RABBITS!
TIM WARNES

More bright and bubbly stories from Little Tiger Press!

For information regarding any of the above titles or for
our catalogue, please contact us:
Little Tiger Press, 1 The Coda Centre,
189 Munster Road, London SW6 6AW
Tel: 020 7385 6333
E-mail: contact@littletiger.co.uk • www.littletiger.co.uk